Dear Beth,
    I'm so grateful for your
friendship! I hope you
    always find wonder in
        the sea and the sky.
                ♡, Jordan

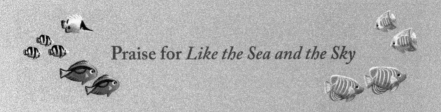

Praise for *Like the Sea and the Sky*

"This sensitive and surprising book illuminates the threads connecting childhood and adulthood, Judaism and science, loneliness, and togetherness. I loved it and you will too."

— Liana Finck, cartoonist for *The New Yorker* and author of *Passing for Human* and *Let There Be Light: The Real Story of Her Creation*

"Seven-year-old Zinni is into marine biology the way many kids her age are into dinosaurs; she even dreams about sea turtles and parrot fish. Zinni is captivated when her mom, a rabbi, tells her about a mollusk found in the Mediterranean that was the source of a beautiful blue dye used on the fringes of prayer shawls. A lovely story about science, imagination, and a joyful spirituality as deep as the blue ocean and as high as the blue sky."

— Anita Diamant, author of *The Red Tent, The Jewish Wedding Now,* and *How to Raise a Jewish Child*

"This beautiful, tender book communicates so much in so few words — about sharing vulnerability, about resilience, about Judaism's expansive approach to learning and thinking — all within exactly the kind of story that kids and parents will return to again and again."

— Rabbi Danya Ruttenberg, author of *Nurture the Wow*

"This book is an utter delight to read. It's a heartwarming story about a mother-daughter relationship, an awe-inspiring account of the natural wonders in the depths of our oceans, and a passionate call to all of us — children and adults alike — to stay curious even when we don't find what we're looking for."

— Sarah Hurwitz, former head speechwriter for First Lady Michelle Obama, and author of *Here All Along: Finding Meaning, Spirituality, and a Deeper Connection to Life — in Judaism (After Finally Choosing to Look There)*

"It is a gift to be reminded of the world's vibrant and mysterious colors. Jordan Namerow has done more in this sweet story than introduce young readers to beautifully woven spiritual traditions, passed down from a wise rabbi to her daughter. *Like the Sea and the Sky* is a well-crafted deep-sea exploration of how to live a grateful life by beginning each day with wonder and growing our souls one blessing at a time."

— Rabbi Menachem Creditor, Scholar in Residence at UJA-Federation of New York, author of *A Rabbi's Heart*

"This lovely tale, a fluid blend of science and religion, inspires wonder for the diverse creatures living underwater — and empathy for those of us living onshore."

— Sigal Samuel, author of *Osnat and Her Dove: The True Story of the World's First Female Rabbi*

"I love this story. It's a wonderful example of how to bring Jewish values and teachings to our children in a loving and supportive way."

— Rabbi Sandra Lawson, Inaugural Director of Racial Diversity, Equity and Inclusion at Reconstructing Judaism

Like the Sea and the Sky

A Mysterious Mollusk and Its Magical Blue Ink

Story by:
Jordan Namerow

Brandylane
Publishers, Inc.
Publishing books since 1985

Art by:
Michelle Simpson

ISBN: 978-1-958754-79-5
Library of Congress Control Number: 2023911992

Designed by Sami Langston
Production managed by Haley Simpkiss

Printed in the United States of America

Published by
Brandylane Publishers, Inc.
5 S. 1st Street
Richmond, Virginia 23219

Brandylane
Publishers, Inc.
Publishing books since 1985

brandylanepublishers.com

For Lior. May you always find wonder in the sea and the sky. And may you stay curious about the past as you dream of the future.

Zinni opened her eyes and peeked at the fringes of her mommy's *tallit* dangling in the morning light. The white and blue knotted threads reminded her of the arms of a jellyfish wriggling through the sea.

"Thank you, God, for helping us wake up and breathe under the sun," her mommy sang in Hebrew.

Zinni's mommy was a rabbi, and every morning she sang the same blessing.

But Zinni didn't usually sing along. Instead, she would daydream about the ocean. Zinni *loved* the ocean and all the interesting things that lived there. Her favorites were mollusks – creatures that had survived in the ocean for over five hundred million years by hiding their squishy bodies inside beautiful shells.

As Mommy lifted her tallit, Zinni peeked out the window and saw the school bus whiz past their house. "Mommy, look!"

"Oh, no. Now I need to drive you to school, Zinni. Let's hurry!" said Mommy.

"Can I stay home from school today?" Zinni asked. There were days when school felt scary. Sometimes letters and numbers got mixed up in her brain, and Zinni was embarrassed to ask for help. Other kids giggled when she asked questions.

"You know, sometimes I don't feel like going to work. Some days, being a rabbi feels scary to me, just like school sometimes feels scary to you," Zinni's mommy shared.

"Like how a sea snail feels when it curls up inside its shell?" Zinni asked.

"Exactly."

Feeling a little better, Zinni quickly brushed her teeth, crammed her jellyfish notebook into her backpack, and raced out to the car.

That afternoon at recess, while the other kids were playing kickball, Zinni doodled different types of mollusks in her jellyfish notebook.

She drew a coconut octopus floating through a kelp forest, and an Atlantic moon snail drilling tiny holes in the sand. She drew herself diving for oysters.

Zinni knew mollusks were special to people all over the world. Her friend, Saya, whose family came from India, had once showed Zinni a photo of her grandpa blowing into the shell of a giant sea snail to make music during a Hindu festival.

It reminded Zinni of blowing the *shofar* for the Jewish New Year. But a shofar isn't a shell. A shofar is the horn of a ram. And a ram is *not* a mollusk.

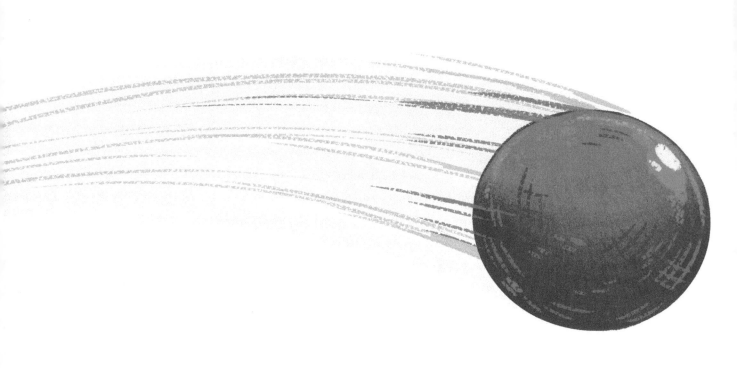

All of a sudden, a kickball bounced over Zinni's notebook, followed by several of her classmates running past. Zinni kept doodling and hoped they wouldn't bother her.

"Hey!" yelled a boy named Aiden as he walked by with the kickball under his arm. "Why are you always drawing silly sea creatures?"

Zinni buried her face in her notebook and didn't answer.

"I bet she wants to be a fish," teased Aiden's friend, Sam. The other kids laughed and made fish faces as Zinni doodled a stingray gliding across the ocean floor.

9

On the bus ride home that day, Zinni pressed her nose against the window and breathed little white clouds onto the glass. She thought about sea creatures with ink sacs that could squirt colorful clouds to scare away predators in the ocean. Sometimes she wished she had her own ink sac to squirt away her fears.

"How was school today?" Mommy asked when Zinni arrived home.

"Fine," Zinni said with a shrug. She pulled her jellyfish notebook out of her backpack and showed Mommy her mollusk doodles.

"You know, I read something cool at work today that reminded me of you," Mommy shared. "See these threads on the fringes of my tallit?"

Zinni nodded and twirled them around her fingers.

"Long ago in ancient times, the color of these threads came from the ink of a mollusk that lived in the Mediterranean Sea."

Zinni's eyes grew large like a squid's.

"No one knows for sure which kind of mollusk made this ink," Mommy continued. "And no one knows its exact color. All we know from our ancient books is that 'the color is like the sea, and the sea is like the sky.'"

Zinni loved the way the sky and the sea swirled together through storms and sunshine – sometimes angry and sad but other times joyful and free.

That night as Zinni drifted off to sleep, she imagined she was floating in the Mediterranean Sea. The turquoise waves felt warm against her skin. She swam past parrot fish and bluefin tunas, past loggerhead turtles and schools of silver sardines. She watched a giant shark gobble up schools of minnows. She plunged deeper and deeper into the ocean to find the ancient mollusk with mysterious ink.

פֶּךְ

Was the ink deep purple-blue like the last part of a sunset? Was it the color of midnight, blue-black behind a glowing crescent moon? Or was it bright like the middle of a sunny day?

הַיָּם

"The color is like the sea, and the sea is like the sky."

In her dream, Zinni swam to a reef with a hundred thousand mollusks. She watched a giant cuttlefish change its skin from fire engine red to dandelion yellow. She saw tiny periwinkles and sea butterflies with sparkly wings float through the sea. She saw ctenophores light up the water with all the colors of the rainbow.

Along an ocean ridge, clusters of shellfish – some shiny, some spikey, some smooth – huddled together, but Zinni could barely tell them apart. Could one of these be the mysterious mollusk?

Zinni swam along the ridge, peering closely at the gleaming shells even though she didn't know what she was looking for. Then, all of a sudden, a cloud of blueish-purple ink surrounded her. It was all she could see. Zinni gasped with amazement. Instead of swallowing saltwater, she breathed in the beautiful color, and it filled her whole body with peace. When the cloud of ink began to fade – as quickly as it had appeared – Zinni felt herself shooting up to the water's surface. She opened her eyes and squinted as the sun outside her window spilled into her room.

It was morning.

"I didn't find it," Zinni mumbled as Mommy kissed her head.

Mommy looked confused. "You didn't find what?"

"I dreamt I was swimming in the Mediterranean Sea. But I couldn't find the ancient mollusk that makes magical blue ink."

Mommy smiled. "You know, we don't always find what we're looking for. What matters is that we keep dreaming, wondering, and trying, even if the answers might never be clear."

Zinni thought about all the salmon swimming upstream on a long, slow journey from saltwater to freshwater to lay their eggs. She thought about the way hermit crabs move into new homes when they outgrow their old ones. She thought about the cuttlefish floating through the ocean in the dark. They were always changing and growing – just like the sea and the sky; just like Mommy and Zinni.

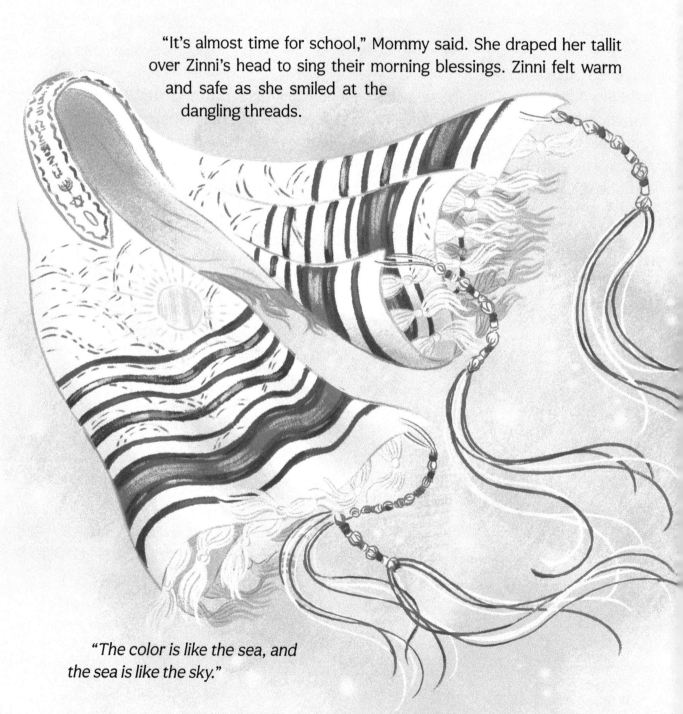

"It's almost time for school," Mommy said. She draped her tallit over Zinni's head to sing their morning blessings. Zinni felt warm and safe as she smiled at the dangling threads.

"The color is like the sea, and the sea is like the sky."

"Thank you, God, who helps our senses distinguish day from night . . . and who gives us freedom, courage, and strength."

She was ready to start a new day.

Author's Note

Thousands of years ago, an ancient sea creature that the Talmud refers to as a *hillazon* produced a blue-colored dye called *tekhelet*. This dye has special significance in Jewish history. *Tekhelet* was used for the robes of Mediterranean kings and princes, and for the *tzitzit* (fringes) of *tallitot* (prayer shawls) that Jewish people wear when they pray. One rabbi from long ago, named Rabbi Meir, wrote, "What is different about *tekhelet* from all other types of colors? *Tekhelet* is like the color of the sea, and the sea is like the sky, and the sky brings us close to God." Scientists and archeologists believe the *hillazon* most closely resembled a sea snail called Murex Trunculus — but we will never know for sure!

24

About the Author

Jordan Namerow is a writer and communications professional. Much of her writing explores themes related to feminism, parenting, social justice, Judaism, and the dynamics of belonging. A graduate of Wellesley College and Columbia University, she lives in Boston with her family. *Like the Sea and the Sky* is Jordan's first children's book. jordannamerow.com

About the Illustrator

Michelle Simpson is a full-time illustrator based out of the Niagara Region of Canada. She graduated with a BAA in illustration from Sheridan College. Michelle's main focus is on children's book illustrations and educational material for kids. She has worked with many large publishing houses and has also created concept artwork and final backgrounds for season two of the children's TV show *Ollie: The Boy Who Became What He Ate* and season one of *Tee and Mo*.

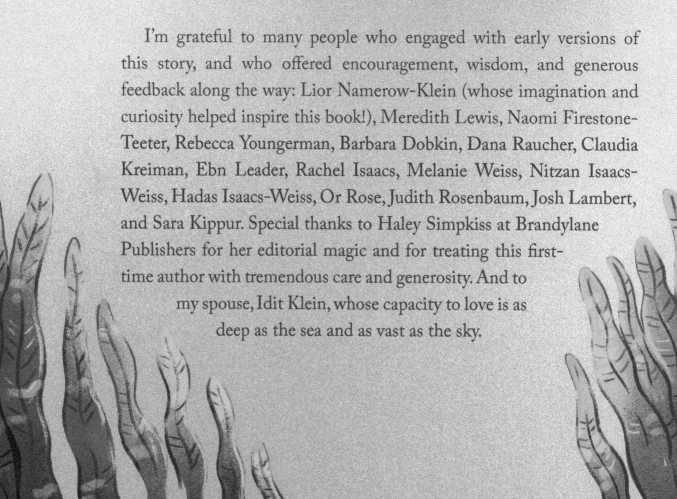

Acknowledgments

I'm grateful to many people who engaged with early versions of this story, and who offered encouragement, wisdom, and generous feedback along the way: Lior Namerow-Klein (whose imagination and curiosity helped inspire this book!), Meredith Lewis, Naomi Firestone-Teeter, Rebecca Youngerman, Barbara Dobkin, Dana Raucher, Claudia Kreiman, Ebn Leader, Rachel Isaacs, Melanie Weiss, Nitzan Isaacs-Weiss, Hadas Isaacs-Weiss, Or Rose, Judith Rosenbaum, Josh Lambert, and Sara Kippur. Special thanks to Haley Simpkiss at Brandylane Publishers for her editorial magic and for treating this first-time author with tremendous care and generosity. And to my spouse, Idit Klein, whose capacity to love is as deep as the sea and as vast as the sky.

Printed in the USA
CPSIA information can be obtained
at www.ICGtesting.com
LVHW072032150823
755351LV00008B/30